AFTER
THE TIDE

Books by Jessie Kwak

AFTER
THE TIDE

JESSIE
KWAK

FAIRWOOD PRESS
Bonney Lake, WA

AFTER THE TIDE
A Fairwood Press Book
Copyright © 2023
by Jessie Kwak

Fairwood Press
21528 104th Street Ct E
Bonney Lake WA 98391

See all our titles at:
www.fairwoodpress.com

ISBN: 978-1-958880-11-1

Fairwood Press First Edition:
August 2023
Also available in ebook

Cover image © 2023 by Zacky Avenged
Cover and book design by Patrick Swenson

Printed in the United States of America

*To anyone who's ever peered
into a tide pool and wondered*

It's the event of the generation, the century, the millennium: all three moons' arms linked in a tug of war to drag the tides low, low—lower. Low enough that the glistening cobbles of Tarry-by-the-Sea's submerged original streets lay naked and exposed tonight for the first time in living memory.

Tonight, the city is alive with revelers accustomed to navigating their city by hovercraft and bridge and gondola and tether-ferry. They walk streets—streets!—littered with debris and rubble, stepping around abandoned watercraft improperly moored, slipping on cobblestones silicone-slick with muck and seaweed. It's filthy, yet here are the gentlefolk out in their nice shoes, ignoring the mud splashing onto the silk and synthetic leather, delighting in the novelty. Three stories above, where the highest tides normally lap twice a day and the above-water portion of the city begins, windows are glazed with kaleidoscopic glass and rimmed with glaring neon and flickering screens; down here it's all been broken out through the centuries since the tides shifted and the original city was washed through to ruin.

Sizzling streetlights fight valiantly to illuminate farther down than usual, and the city's ubiquitous cameras, too, struggle to pierce the gloom. To fill the gap in security, drones drift overhead, quietly humming, made innocuous and cheerful with chains of bright paper lanterns strung between them, the light reflecting off the puddles and glossy-wet cobbles in a shattered neon rainbow.

Bands thrum beats into the newly-uncovered plazas, the ferrymen—their gondolas dry-docked tonight, their hovercraft unneeded—offer to guide revelers on tours of the lower levels. Giant sentry spiders, normally confined to rooftops and bridge decks, stalk the streets on spindly, robotic legs. Someone's tied a bright nylon scarf around the leg of this one, the single unblinking eye in its belly whirs as it scans the crowd, shutter clicking at a suspicious face. It continues on.

The residents of the city's lower half have taken cover as the residents of the upper half descend, but not all can hide. Barnacles, mussels, limpets encrust the stone walls, unable to run as enterprising foragers pry them off to be served on the night's specials menus. Anemone clamp tight and sandy and sullen against the prodding fingers of toddlers, waiting desperately to unfurl when the tide comes in again. Crabs peer out from under crumbling walls, minnows flounder in the dwindling tidepools, splashed about by revelers.

They're not the only ones left vulnerable tonight.

But. Peer inside the shadows beyond the upper crust's gaiety and the tidal resident's misery, and you'll find an entirely different sort of game finishing up as the tide rises once more: a three-hour span of hallucinatory frenzy that was touted as the game of the generation, the century, the millennium. It's over, and now—victorious?—Adria stands over Pandora's smoking body with an empty gun in her hand and nowhere left to run.

Wait.
I went too fast.
Let's give that another go.

Same story about the trio of moons and the historic tide, same poetical waxing about the citizens of the city coming down to gawk at the denizens of the deep—but I'll put three hours back on the clock.

Same crowds, same frantic festival energy with bands soundwashing the plazas, the enterprising ferrymen and fastidious sentry spiders working the crowds. Someone's tied a bright nylon scarf around the leg of this one, and Adria ducks underneath it to avoid a clutch of giggling society toffs, glancing up at the single unblinking eye in its belly. It whirs as it focuses on her face, then clicks and keeps moving, ignored by the rest of the crowd.

She's on her way to the game of her generation, the century, the millennium, driven by curiosity and obligation and the wooden box in her pack—which has no right to feel as heavy as it is, given the objectively light weight of the contents. The game was advertised to its exclusive audience as an unmissable event, one where anything goes and all traces of the rules, the too-slow participants, the blood, will be washed away after the tide comes back in.

Adria has a few things she intends to leave behind for the tide.

(I know this now; when the game began, although I knew every fact about her—about all of them—I could only guess at her secret thoughts. Now, I find it impossible to separate Adria's memories of this tale from my own.)

She slips through a broken doorway

and into an abandoned courtyard, sky empty of drones and gaping wide to reveal brilliant triple moons. A small pack has gathered, all scenting blood and waiting to hear the rules of the game. There are no waivers to sign, no place to put your name. No recording devices, no media, no broadcasting, no uploading your successes to the feeds.

And no glory for the winner, but I haven't told them that, not yet.

It's a motley crowd, Adria thinks. Of course Techs are here, showing off their hardware mods, a knot of them swapping stats on cybernetic implants, muscle bulkers, oxygen boosters. No one knows the rules so tech isn't cheating—but that doesn't mean the game's non-outwardly modded contestants will like them here. Everything else in this topsy-turvy world may be upside down tonight, but that prejudice stays the same.

Most of the other participants are who Adria would expect: street toughs and hustlers and more than a few low-level con artists like Adria herself; she exchanges a few guarded nods with her colleagues, keeps a wary eye out for past marks.

Not that they'd recognize her today. Her targets are generally corporate: her costume is heels, wigs, lipstick, and tight-fitting business suits that show off her athletic frame and siphon cognitive resources from her marks. Tonight her stocking cap is pulled low over her spiked bleached hair. She's wearing dark gray joggers and a cheap black stealth jacket, carrying a black nylon canvas pack with the square outline of its contents ghosting against the fabric.

"Who're those ones, then?"

A quiet voice at Adria's shoulder startles her out of her scan of the crowd, and she turns to find a slight man with cool olive skin and dark eyes, dressed more like a tourist from the society streets than the sort of riff-raff Adria expected to see here.

"Pardon?"

The man lifts his chin to a group at the edge of the crowd: they're not wearing uni-forms but they might as well be by the stiff, uncomfortable way they hold themselves. The big one with the pale complexion, fierce braid, and hooked nose is the leader; the rest are watching her for orders, attuned like a pack of trained wolves.

"Corporate security?" Adria guesses, though what the hell would they be doing here?

"Here to shut this down?" her companion muses in answer to her unasked question. "Though they're not alone."

Adria follows his gaze and realizes he's right. Another clutch of game-players have gathered at the far end of the courtyard. While the first set—Adria mentally names them wolves—are stiff and disciplined, this other corporate security team are languid as tigers, their leader lounging against the wall with his shirt half-unbuttoned and blond hair tousled, going for the look of an underworld playboy though he hasn't bothered to hide his corporate-issue sleeve. The leader of the tigers catches her looking and gives a wink.

"Here to play," Adria says, and her

companion nods.

"Here to ruin it for the rest of us."

The wolves and the tigers eye each other across the courtyard, clearly bristling at each other's presence.

"Let them try," Adria says.

Her companion laughs. "I like that." He holds out a hand. "Logan."

A flurry of aliases on her tongue, but she bites them back. Tonight is different. Special. The first night of a new life where she isn't defined by her mark, or her father, or anything else in this blaze-damned city.

"Adria," she says; the syllables taste strange.

"Nice to meet you. Any idea what this is about?"

"Nope."

"Good. Me neither." Logan tilts a meaningful look at the pack over her shoulder. "Were we meant to have brought a pack? I didn't think to."

"No—I mean, I don't know." Color flares in Adria's cheeks. "It's kind of a personal thing."

Something about her tone must clue Logan in to the depth of pain behind tonight's quest; something in the way his expression gentles sparks a sudden desire in Adria to explain herself.

"My father," she says, patting the pack even while knowing that's insufficient explanation. "He'd been looking forward to this night, you know? But he didn't make it. So I thought I'd bring him."

"His ashes," Logan says, soft.

Adria feels a rush of relief that Logan didn't tell her he was sorry for her loss—she's not. At least, not the way she's probably supposed to be. Her father may have finally drank himself to death two months back, but she lost the man she loved years ago. If that dull ache in her chest is grief, it's long been scabbed over.

"He would have loved this," she says.

And he would have: the mystery, the pageantry, the ridiculous secretive nature of the game, the chance to explore the city.

"This city's in our blood, Ad," he'd told her, but lately it's felt like a cage, titanium chain link woven out of *his* memories and *his* expectations and his tangle of aliases and backstories and confidence games that she can hardly keep straight anymore.

Adria needs to find herself, and she won't do it here. She's been trying to leave Tarry-by-the-Sea for years, ever since her father started drinking in earnest, but she kept finding obstacles in her way. The timing of a job offer didn't work out. Opportunities fell through. For years now there's been something sluggish in her preparations, some maddening internal reluctance she couldn't quite pinpoint and couldn't quite barrel past, and although she doesn't believe in fate or greater powers, something—don't call it the universe, call it the City—seemed to be standing in her way.

It wasn't her father, he's been ashes in a box for months and she still hasn't walked away. She'd wondered if she'd need to take him with her, but then she remembered the low tide was coming and she'd known what to do. When she heard about the game it felt like the perfect piece of the puzzle.

This is just the ridiculous sort of shit her father had lived for, before he'd lived for the bottle. She'll take him with her, and handful by handful she'll say goodbye and be on her way. She has her shuttle ticket for tomorrow evening. Her bags are packed. After tonight, Adria—not an alias, not a con, but *Adria*—is heading out into the world to freedom.

Someone has climbed a small flight of steps at the north end of the courtyard, voice mods sending their words echoing off the dripping walls and silencing the crowd.

It's time.

I hold my metaphorical breath.

"Welcome!" The speaker is barrel chested and fit, wide shock of blue-dyed curls piled high. "The game will begin in a few minutes, as soon as everyone receives their welcome packet. It includes your personalized instructions, as well as what your bonus will be if you win."

"I thought the prize was cash," shouts someone near the front.

The speaker smiles. "That, and so much more."

A murmur as that sinks over the crowd: anticipation, delight, unease.

A chill touches Adria's neck. She's not hung up on what the prize *is*, she's hung up on the word "personalized." Who the hell knows she's here? Adria turns to Logan to ask what the speaker means, but a figure in a red jumpsuit steps between them, pressing a tool roll of plasticized canvas into each of their outstretched hands before moving on.

The speaker's voice booms again. "You may share what you learn in your packet with anyone you wish, or no one at all. The game will last three hours. You'll know it's over when this courtyard is underwater once more."

Adria shares a confused glance with Logan, then unties the roll to reveal a pearl-handled blade, a shimmering vial, a leaden disk, a cheap plastic lighter, each in their own pocket. A scrap of reusable newsprint falls from the parcel; she reacts quickly, scooping the fluttering chit out of the air with clawed fingers before it can land in the muck at her feet.

She smooths it open in her hand, shielding it from view.

A seedling from Cambie Downs intertwines with a cutting from the Golden Forest and an orchid from the Seathe Coast. My roots run deeper than you know, as tangled a maze as my branches.

The lines are labeled "Clue." The words begin to flicker on the newsprint as she frowns at them, pixels swarming and resolving into a new message, labeled "Prize."

I know who you really are.

Adria crumples the newsprint in her fist reflexively; she risks a glance to see Logan with the same strange set of tools and his own scrap of newsprint. His brows draw together as he reads it, a flicker of complicated emotion—hope, maybe, or grief?—in his eyes before he carefully folds the scrap away.

Are their clues the same? Their prizes? Should she ask? Given the silence from around the courtyard, the rest of the players are keeping their clues close to the vest. She slips the crumpled newsprint into the pocket of her joggers, but the final message tolls through her mind like a ship's bell through the fog.

I know who you really are.

It could be a threat, a sign that she should walk away from this game right now. But it could also be a promise. And that golden barb sticks in her soul more deeply than any cash prize possibly could.

The speaker at the front calls for attention once more. "Any questions about the rules?"

"Yes!" a joker shouts back. "What are they?"

Nervous laughter from around the courtyard; the person who yelled out the question isn't alone in their confusion.

"You'll know," says the speaker. And lifts a hand, clutching a wicked shape that hitches Adria's breath, but it's only a flare gun—still, when the speaker shoots into the air the crowd below startles with screams that are half delight, half genuine shock. Sparks cascade over them like scattered petals.

"Sure way to call security," mutters Logan beside her, and seconds later Adria can hear the whine of drones over the hubbub of the crowd. Any moment sentry spiders will come crawling over the rooftops and descend to reel in order. The tall speaker, the rest of the organizers, they're already running. Adria pockets the pearl-handled knife, shoves the rest of her new tool roll into her pack along with the ash-filled box.

"Good luck," she calls to Logan. The wolf pack's hook-nosed chief shouts for her team to follow her; the tigers slip languidly after their tousled playboy leader.

The game is on, and Adria and the other contestants scatter like rats into the maze of buildings in the City-beneath-the-City, feet squelching in seaweed, skin pricking with adrenaline and fear and anticipation and greed.

Adria knows exactly where she's going and why: the Sevenwood Botanical Garden, to find out who she really is.

Adria's father used to tell her stories, back when an evening pint or two put him in a storytelling mood, before they became afternoon pints and morning pints and he could no longer remember the stories that had once danced through his mind.

"Ad, did I ever tell you about the labyrinth under the botanical garden?" He began the story—The Beast of the Labyrinth—one night when they sat together under the stars in a darker, quieter part of the city, watching the starlight glitter off lapping waves of the canals. Adria has always assumed it was mostly his fancy. She'll find out soon enough which parts are true.

Back then, Adria had lain awake for hours while he unspooled threads of legend into the night. Now, snatches of memory flicker back as she approaches Sevenwood—or, rather, the barnacle-encrusted ancient stone walls that support the island the botanical garden occupies.

Three stories above, foot bridges arch gracefully overhead. She's crossed them herself. At high tide the water glimmers barely a meter below the bridges, sometimes blooming with schools of jellyfish, sometimes flashing with minnows, sometimes haunted by darker, swifter shadows.

Tonight, the bridges sketch dark lines against the moon-bright sky. The jellyfish and minnows have retreated to safer waters; the darker, swifter shadows remain on the fringes of Adria's vision, slipping through the reveling crowd to find their marks.

Adria slips through the crowd, too, skirting the island of Sevenwood, following that thread her father set adrift in her mind so many years ago. *My roots run deeper than you know, as tangled a maze as my branches*. She doesn't know where the rest of the game's participants have gone, and she's not sure she recognizes any of them among the crowd here; Sevenwood's stewards are hosting a sort of educational program to discuss the garden's history.

"How do I get in?" she mutters under her breath, but if the ashes in her pack can hear her, they certainly can't answer.

But, there: a door rusted with centuries of salt, chained shut but so tide-battered that one side has been prised free from its hinges and shoved askew, just wide enough that Adria can slip through if she takes her pack off.

Tide-battered? Or simply battered; Adria notes the dents seemed hammered into the door from the *inside*, deep gouges scoring metal and stone. The animal part of Adria's mind sends out warning. The higher-evolved part does that uniquely human risk calculation I admire, the one heavily—and falsely—weighted with naive hope for the best.

Adria pushes through the door and does not look back.

Last year, Adria sprang for a pair of eye implants after a particularly good payday, and upgraded them to include a night vision mod when she heard about this game. But she didn't spend much time getting used to them and it's not as simple as turning night into day. The flat colors, sizzling greens, blazes of heat—she whips her head around to follow a flash of movement and finds a crab scuttling into a dripping cranny. Her boots splash in shallow puddles reeking with tidal silt. In the darkness, something is tapping, rhythmic. Adria hopes it's dripping water, but still she pulls the pearl-handled knife from her pocket and flicks open the blade.

Another step, another puddle splash with driftwood shifting under her boots, but the path is sloping gently up and Adria is soon out of the water and walking the path of—oh. Not driftwood, then.

She suppresses a shudder.

She's in a sort of catacomb, the bones long washed from their nooks and covering the floor in a knobby carpet of femurs and ribs. She can't decide if it's better or worse that the catacomb's builders removed the skulls and cemented them to the walls—she won't have to step on them, but they'll be watching her tread on their discarded skeletons, their bones bleached clean long before the sea swept into the city and filled the passageways.

Adria keeps walking, looking for her next clue. Riddles are inscribed over funereal niches, but they're all ancient, mere epitaphs of names and dates in outdated script and lost languages. One of the niches catches her eye: a stone chalice carved into the cave wall, surrounded by carved stone fruit. It's ridiculous, and she imagines her father laughing at the cornucopia of bananas and pomegranates and figs.

Her *old* father would have laughed, at least. She'd never known how the man who finally died of drink would react.

When the water returns he'll get a chance to explore the entire system of catacombs on the eddying currents of churning waves, but this is a fitting place to start the journey. Adria unzips her pack, unlatches the box, hesitates. Fitting, the ashes in the catacomb? Or is it too on the nose? Should she scatter the whole box? Or save some to carry with her out of the City so he can see more of the universe than this choked corner?

She finally decides that her father would find the idea of ashes in the catacombs amusing—and that if he wanted to take his own adventure down in the City-beneath-the-City he would have found a way to sober up enough to live to this night.

She tips a handful of ash into the carved chalice, latches the box once more, and keeps walking with her step slightly lighter. Metacarpals skitter off the scuffing toes of her boots, but their echo is eerily out of rhythm with her own footsteps. Adria pauses, listening. She's not the only one stirring up old bones tonight.

The passageway widens into a small room, and something shifts in the corner. A gentle huffing sound, no sea creature she's ever heard of; Adria whips around to find the source of the noise amid the smear of electric pea green. Before she can, the thing charges.

Hulking, leaping, hooves splintering bone—the Beast of the Labyrinth knocks

Adria to the ground and pins her between its horns. Its breath sears from its snout, fetid and rotting and metallic with fresh kill.

Adria lies perfectly still, trying to breathe as little—and as quietly—as possible.

The Beast snorts again, pulls back. Tosses its head. Speaks:

"Why are you here?"

Adria swallows: dry tongue, parched throat. The Beast is human, she realizes. Metal horns and protruding facial implants and a neck thick with braided wiring. A Tech gone so machine she'd think them a construct if not for the warmth of their body.

"Why are you here?" the Beast demands once more.

"My father told me stories about you," she says.

"And that didn't make you stay away?"

"I didn't think you were real."

"I bleed as real as you do, don't I?" And at that, the Beast sits back. Pulls the pearl-handled knife from their thigh with a grunt, wipes it on their robes and hands it to her, handle-first. Adria hadn't even realized it was still in her hand when the Beast charged.

"I'm sorry," she stammers. "I didn't mean—"

The Beast huffs away her apology. "Choked with coral, tonight we breathe."

"What?"

"Your next riddle, little human." The Beast clambers into a crouch, hoof-feet crunching bone, the golden ring through their nostrils sparking in Adria's night vision.

"Wait," she says, when the Beast turns to leave. "What's the point of all these riddles?"

The Beast twitches tattered priest's robes over furred haunches. "Pandora will tell you," they call over their shoulder. "If you can find her."

Adrenaline kicks in as soon as the Beast vanishes through another open passage, and Adria scrambles over silt-slick tibia and scapula to her feet. She snatches up her pack and runs panting back to the entrance in case the Beast changes their mind and decides to gore her anyway. Pulls her way through the door shaking and sweating, and not until she's back in the fresher air of the rotting tides does her mind register what the Beast told her.

Choked with coral, tonight we breathe.

She climbs a set of stairs worn soft and rounded, slippery with ancient grime, and perches on a balcony with her back against a serrated mat of barnacles. Lets her heart rate ebb, and opens her pack.

It was all part of the game she tells herself, and she pulls the tool roll out to explore the contents more fully while her mind mulls over the words.

Choked with coral, tonight we breathe.

The cheap plastic lighter: maybe she should have used that in the labyrinth, maybe she would have if she hadn't had the night vision implant.

The leaden disc: she turns it over in her fingers, searching for an etching, a sign. Nothing.

The shimmering vial: ah. It suddenly

strikes her what this is. Zephyr, a hallucinatory drug. Daredevils use it for the rush of breathing underwater, it floods your veins with enough oxygen to keep you alive and enough of a drug cocktail to give you an incredible high—the sensory experience and hallucinations are apparently amazing. If you keep your wits about you and get out of the water in time.

What the fuck, Adria thinks. What the fuck.

For what won't be the first time tonight, she thinks she should quit the game, just explore the City-beneath-the-City and scatter some ashes and buy a twist of candy floss and watch the street performers with the rest of the crowds. But, as bizarre as the labyrinth was, the Beast didn't actually try to hurt her.

It *is* only a game—a game which became something much more as soon as she saw that note:

I know who you really are.

At least someone does, thinks Adria, and if they do, she needs to find out, too.

And besides. Her mind, mulling these past minutes while she rested, has unknotted the answer to the minotaur's riddle.

She picks her way down the stairs, then melts into shadow as she sees the wolf pack arriving, led by their fiercely braided leader. The pack pry open the door and file in as she barks orders. Are they just now solving the riddle of the labyrinth below Sevenwood, or have they been to another stop before this? No way to tell if each player was given a unique sequence of stops, so Adria starts to jog, picking her way through the maze of streets and revelers and pick-pockets and secretive crabs and traumatized anemone and dying minnows.

She's heading to the reef.

Excellent.

I considered various ways to harness the energy of the revelers tonight; surely their frenetic carousing through the streets could be captured, transmuted into electricity? Each of my proposed inventions was more fanciful than the last, each woefully inefficient and riddled with failure points I couldn't control. In the end I went with a more mundane solution: enormous battery packs, carefully secured.

It's a calculated risk.

My network draws tremendous power, which I usually attain by tapping the undulations of the ocean, underwater turbines harnessing tidal energy throughout the City-beneath-the-City. The new batteries—large as they are—have only enough reserves to animate my necessaries, and only for a few hours. But by the time the tides return this game should have come to its conclusion, and I should be safe.

I'm keeping a metaphorical eye on my dwindling power supply as Adria darts through the streets to the reef, where the underwater sculpture garden—a paradise for human divers and cephalopod explorers alike—is now partially exposed, the heads of the ever-drowning figures above water for these few brief hours. Adria knows this city well, it seems. Other players have been less quick to decipher my riddles, but they're still advancing. My enemies quicker than most.

I watch them all and learn, because that is my way. I never stop learning, growing, educating myself.

Tonight I am learning what it is to be helpless, vulnerable.

Tonight I am learning fear.

A fter the horrors of the catacombs, Adria finds the challenge at the reef simple enough. A logic puzzle quickly solved; when she's chosen the correct coral-encrusted statue she turns to find a ragged mechanical pelican with a scarred eye and a blank scroll cradled in its beak. Adria thanks it for the scroll, then frowns at the empty paper a moment before deciding to employ the cheap plastic lighter. Success: as the edges of the scroll curl back, the next clue—*SALISHA*—is illuminated letter by letter. Charred paper drifts into the tidepools at her feet, along with another handful of her father's ashes and a word of grudging thanks to him.

Because if not for her father, Adria might not know about the *Salisha*. She learned of it through his stories, his morbid fascination with the many shipwrecks dotting the rocky coast that surrounds Tarry-by-the-Sea's harbor. The *Salisha* went down in his youth, a smuggler's ship with a sordid history, sinking at the mouth of the harbor with a presumed cargo of gold and treasure. The treasure's gone, of course. The shipwreck's location wasn't a mystery and its bones have been picked clean by divers over the past forty years. Tonight, as the *Salisha* lays exposed once more to the night air, it's not a destination for revelers, not like the dowdy and well-storied wreck of the *Sweet Aline* with its grand staircases and shattered crystal chandeliers. Someone's organized a soiree at the *Sweet Aline* tonight, complete with a temporary dancing platform and a musical quartet; Adria picks her way through the muddy harbor in the opposite direction of the festivities.

At the *Salisha*, Adria makes quick work of the challenge, which is to walk along the tilted ship's deck without sliding the entire wreck off its fulcrum point. Adria's always been light on her feet, nimble, even though the staccato splashing in the tide below—is the tide rising now? it is—tells her something every child in the city learns by heart from an early age. Water snakes, a mere hand's span below the exposed deck.

The puzzle at the end of the challenge is just as neatly solved: each identical gold coin on its own pressure plate a perfect match for the lead disk in her tool roll. Her fingers are quick enough to trade with one without upsetting the pressure plate and startling the snake that sits coiled and wary, fangs glinting in the moonlight.

And then she's off the ruined *Salisha* and gone to roost on the top of a nearby broken wall, tucked out of sight, mulling over the riddle on the coin a long while as she watches other players approach the wreck. A handful see the snakes and incoming tide and decide this game is no longer for them. Whatever prize was scrawled on their scrap of newsprint wasn't enough.

One, though, presses on. She recognizes him as the man, Logan, who spoke to her at the beginning.

She watches Logan even after her mind finally clicks the riddle into place, pinned to her roost with mounting worry as the rising tide begins to unbalance the *Salisha's* deck even further. A water snake with visions of dinner has become bold, looped its coils to pull its lithe body from the water and tip the deck just as Logan reaches the gold coins.

"Watch out!" Adria calls before she realizes she's going to—Logan glances back, but there's nothing he can do to keep the ship from tilting. Adria acts without thinking, hauling back her arm and loosing the coin in her hand like a stone; it strikes the water snake soundly in the head and the dazed creature slides back off the platform and into the sea, righting the deck and giving Logan a chance to escape.

A pang at the loss of the valuable coin, but Adria tells herself (correctly) that even though it was real gold, keeping it probably came at a higher cost. It might have had a tracking device, she thinks (correctly). A sinister plan from the authorities to find any lowlifes who decided to play this game, she wonders (incorrectly).

And anyway, she's already solved the riddle. The words inscribed on the edge were written in a language none still speak, but she finally realized it wasn't so much the ancient phrase that signified but its acrostic: *BATHS*. Though, of course, the language should have been a clue.

Logan has made his way off the platform and is searching to see who shouted warning and threw the coin, but Adria is already running, a handful of ash drifting down from the wall she'd perched on.

Her father finally gets to explore the wreck he always wanted to see with his own eyes. Adria's off to the ruins of the sacrificial baths, her pack—and soul—lighter and lighter.

The moons may have pulled the tides low, lower, but even this historic confluence hasn't managed to uncover the absolute lowest levels of this ancient city. The sacrificial baths are one of many ruins of the civilization that made this harbor its home before Tarry-by-the-Sea was founded and the waters rose. Archaeologists have studied the baths, the massive stone columns and ceremonial urns that serve purposes no one remembers, comparing them to similar sites found in areas where the tides don't reach. In these other sites, the ceremonial urns are ritually stained black with what scholars assume was human blood.

Anyone who comes here tonight will get a chance to see the baths as they were when the ancients used them for unknown purposes: the raised tile platform surrounding a central pool, carved stone steps descending into the murky waters. Maybe back in those time-worn days the water in the pool was clear and pure; tonight it's black and soupy as ink.

Archaeologists have swam these halls, explored the buildings surrounding the sacrificial baths, but no one has plumbed the depths of the pool itself. Even this lowest of low tides hasn't laid its secrets bare to the moonlight tonight.

When Adria arrives, she's preoccupied with the quickly rising tide and realizes—too late—that, this time, she's not first on the scene. The tousled blond playboy with the corporate sleeve and his pride of languid tigers are here already, prowling the baths in search of the next clue.

Adria crouches in the shadows as soon as she notices the tigers, but her approach was hardly stealthy and one of the pride was waiting for her. Iron grip wrenching her arms behind her back, he hauls her out into the wash of moonlight that pours through the building's broken roof. Adria stumbles forward with a yelp, and the tousled playboy leader looks up from the inscription he's examining, tilts his head to study Adria instead.

His eyes flash, glimmering silver lines of his implants sparking moonlight like dew in a spider's web, so cold that fear spikes through Adria's heart—until he smiles, and his eyes are all warmth again, and she wonders if she imagined the previous calculating chill.

The air in the ruins reeks of death—the sea is the largest graveyard in the world, isn't it—and Adria can't keep her mind from reeling through the stories her father told her about the ancients and their blood sacrifices, acts so brutal the tides rose to wash the entire civilization away. She's dizzy with imagination. That can't possibly be the final challenge, human sacrifice? She hopes the grisly possibility hasn't occurred to the tigers.

This is only a game, she reminds herself, and these are just a corporate security team, not some murderous band of underworld assassins. It's only a game, but:

I know who you really are.

"Oh, hello," the tigers' leader says brightly, a wink and toss of his chin at his underling to let Adria free. "I saw you at the start. I'm Grisholm."

He doesn't introduce any of his other corporate security tigers, who surround her and Grisholm together with weapons out but not aimed. Grisholm ignores them; Adria keeps a wary eye on them.

"I'm Adria," she says.

"Nice to meet you, Adria." Grisholm turns, sweeping his gaze over the ruins. She wonders what those implants allow him to see, they look much more expensive than hers. "Now. What do you suppose we're supposed to do here?"

"I don't know." After a frustrating evening of maddening riddles on her own, it's almost nice to have someone else to speculate with. As long as she ignores the toughs bristling with weapons around her. "The challenges at the other locations haven't been exactly clear."

"And yet you've solved them all so

far, and on your own. I'm impressed." Grisholm's sly wink carries heat; Adria's cheeks warm.

One of his tigers crouches beside a broken urn, playing light over the glyphs on the side. "Every one of these inscriptions are ancient," the tiger says, frowning back at Grisholm. "The statue puzzle, the gold coins, the hand-to-hand combat in the catacombs—those puzzles were all front and center. Are you sure we're in the right place?"

"And what's the point of all these riddles?" asks another, shining a torch at the surface of the pool. The light penetrates mere centimeters into the gloom before being swallowed up.

What's the point of all these riddles is the very question Adria had asked the Beast of the Labyrinth earlier, and the Beast had answered:

"Pandora will tell us if we can find her," Adria says.

Electric silence sizzles through the air.

"And what do you know about Pandora?" Grisholm asks. His tone is still light, but something in his stance has changed, sharpened.

"Nothing. That's just what the Beast said."

Grisholm gestures to one of his tigers, and rough hands strip the pack from Adria's back before she realizes what's about to happen.

"Stop," she yells, clawing for the bag, but another tiger grabs her tight, locking her in the iron bands of his arms. The emptying of her bag happens quickly, there's not much to pull out. The tool roll, with only the vial of Zephyr remaining, is dropped to the tile floor in favor of examining the wooden box. "Leave that alone!"

Grisholm ignores her and holds out his hand for the box, turning it over with a frown before unlatching it. A trickle of ash spills to the floor, leaving barely enough for Adria to take with her when she leaves the city. Ash clings to Grisholm's damp fingertips. Adria's heart clenches, grief and rage.

"What the fuck is this?"

"My father," Adria snarls, and his eyes go wide. Grisholm closes the box quickly, latches it again carefully. Jerk of his chin releases Adria from his muscled underling's grasp once more, and Grisholm hands back the box.

"Explain."

"He died a few months back," Adria says, heart still pounding. "The game was a good excuse to scatter his ashes. A final sendoff."

"And you know nothing about Pandora."

"I don't know anything, the Beast just said the name." Somehow the night has taken a dark, sharp-edged turn. The moons have dropped low on the horizon, casting jagged shadows over the ruins and the strange seabed landscape they had joined forces to so graciously uncover and illuminate. Part of Adria wants nothing more than to scamper back home, take a scalding shower, and burrow into bed. But even if Grisholm does believe her and send her on her way, that golden barb of desperate curiosity won't let her quit the game.

I know who you really are.

Before Grisholm can answer, a woman's shout slices through the night. Voices in the distance, barked orders, moving closer. Grisholm's jaw sets.

"Coronata's here," he says, annoyed, and draws a pistol from his belt.

The wolves are closing in, and Adria's about to be caught in the middle of a clash between the two corporate security teams that are inexplicably here to play a game Adria needs to win. She clutches the wooden box to her chest, ready to rabbit, but there's no way out. The wolves have them surrounded.

She and the tigers will be driven out of the ruins, just like the ancients who built these sacrificial baths had been driven out in her father's stories by the people who had eventually built Tarry-by-the-Sea. In the stories her father used to make up—make up?—the reason the archaeologists don't know what happened to the ancients is that they developed gills and swam away to sea.

Oh, no, she thinks. That *can't* be it.

Around Adria, knives and gun barrels flash in the moonlight, shouted orders echoing off the stone columns, targeting lasers painting points that seem to sizzle against the damp. The rising tide pulses the level of the black pool in the center of the baths, sloshing seawater over Adria's shoes, and before she can second guess herself she bends down to snatch the vial of Zephyr from her tool roll. She downs it in a swallow, light and glory flaring down her throat and blooming through her chest, streaks of fire spreading through her veins.

And she dives-tumbles-falls into the pool with the wooden box clutched in one hand, feet kicking hard to get away from the battle as the first bullets begin to chip stone. Her night vision illuminates—just barely—the darker tunnel carved into the tile floor of the pool. She swims toward it, lungs aching, hoping against hope that the tunnel is short.

It's not.

She holds her breath until her lungs

nearly burst, until her vision dims, until she has no choice but to test whether or not Zephyr actually does allow you to breathe underwater. Her lungs scream fire when they fill with brine, but the burn ebbs quickly, and clarity rushes back into her mind along with a spark of color and light.

She breathes out, expelling brine in a flurry of bubbles. Breathes back in, fascinated.

The part of her mind that is still somewhat coherent notes that either Zephyr works, or she's flying so high that she doesn't know she's actually dying. Even if it's the latter, the tunnel has ended and she's blown away by the brilliance.

It's amazing down here.

She's not in the murky tomb she'd expected, but in a swirling, kaleidoscope world of stained glass and brilliance. Schools of silver fish flash by, anemones glow neon, fronds pulsing and sticky as they close around her fingers then bloom again to catch the bounty of the tides.

She shouldn't linger—she has no

idea how long this drug will last—but it's impossible to tell what's up and down. Windows are everywhere, every shadow a potential door, and as she searches for an exit the hand that's not holding her father's wooden box keeps reaching for what looks like freedom and finding solid wall. Someone's speaking to her, voice liquid and distant, and she slowly realizes that the stained glass windows she's been admiring are actually screens. Their images refract rainbows in the current, glorious. Adria wafts her free hand in the water, spinning slowly, entranced by the effect.

"Let him go," I say. Adria gapes at my screens, and I repeat: "Let him go."

I keep talking, a strange sensation that might be panic rising as my batteries drain until Adria finally blinks free of the Zephyr—and her memories of her father—long enough to close both hands around the wooden box. Fingers fumble for the clasp, and her father's remaining ashes drift from the shallows of the container like glittering snow. Does the cloud of ash transform into her father's face a moment, blissful smile of release, or is it the same as laying back on a rooftop, staring up at the clouds—that one's a rabbit, that one's a water snake, that one's the Beast Under the City—Adria blinks, trying to pull herself out of the revery, but she's too far gone into the drug.

Maybe she should enjoy the way the minnows seem to dance before her, maybe she should enjoy the fractured rainbows, maybe she should enjoy the golden glow of fireflies gathering in the small box that once held her father's ashes.

She smiles down at them and they blink, flash, hundreds of tiny lights, thousands of individual glittering conversations she's not invited into. She remembers magical childhood evenings capturing them one at a time in the marshes, and now here she has a thousand golden fireflies all in one go . . .

She closes the box reverently to keep the fireflies safe and latches it while the currents drift around her.

The voice from the screens is still

speaking, nonsense numbers—*seven-six-zero-four-eight, seven-six-zero-four-eight*—that she ignores because the screens are flickering out, now, one at a time, showers of sparks which shouldn't be possible underwater, but anything's possible in a dream.

She's not dreaming.

Adrenaline finally spikes through the haze of the hallucination, and for a moment Adria's vision clears, the many screens and windows shifting into one for a brief second before shattering into duplicate triplicate multitudes once more. She tries to fix the direction in her shifting mind, tries to send signals of motion to her pleasantly numb limbs, and finally the next time she places her hand on a window it finds an exit. She pulls herself through, the burning in her lungs a new sensation, one she starts to recognize means the drug is wearing off and she's got only a few seconds left of this unnatural ability not to breathe.

Hopefully that means the hallucination is wearing off, too. She pulls herself through another window, it's easier to find them now, and then another, and suddenly she breaks the surface with salt-blinded eyes—she gasps with lungs bursting and bitter brine on her tongue, in her nose, hand clawing for purchase and finding an escape ladder slimed with seaweed. Her fingers slip, grasp, slip again, catch, too exhausted, but before she falls back into the pool her hand grasps another's.

Strong arms pull her gasping like a fish onto the cold stone floor, where she coughs until her lungs ache and her throat is fire, until she can finally breathe without rasping. Something's digging painfully into her ribs—the wooden box which she's miraculously and stupidly managed to cling to. Adria shifts her weight off it and looks up to find her rescuer.

Logan.

"You okay?"

She nods, still coughing, not trusting her voice to work. Logan's squatting beside her, giving her space. His clothes are soaking wet, too, she realizes, and she wonders in panic if there's a way to get here that doesn't involve a marathon swim fueled by psychedelics. (There is.)

"What happened?" he asks, and when Adria can finally breathe and speak at the same time she tells him: seeing him at the *Salisha*, scaring away the water snake, arriving at the sacrificial baths to find the tigers, the arrival of the wolves, and her realization that the final challenge was to dive into the baths.

"Bastards," Logan says. "Do you think any of them followed you?"

"I don't know." Adria pushes herself back to sit against a wall, finally studying the room she's emerged in. A cement-walled bunker from some forgotten war, the square pool Logan hauled her out of designed to house submersibles, maybe. Logan's lit a lantern, but the flame isn't the only flickering light illuminating the dark. A control panel built into the wall is blinking red with error: *INCORRECT CODE*.

"Where are we?" Adria asks. "Did you swim here, too?"

Logan shakes his head. "There's a way in from the stairs at the base of the lighthouse. I used to dive here when I was younger and explore these bunkers."

Adria glances at the control panel. "Was that always there?"

A smile ghosts across Logan's lips. "No."

"So you think that's the last puzzle?"

"Maybe. I was trying to guess at the code, but then I remembered the Zephyr, and realized maybe the only way to get the code was to take it and dive into the water. I was just steeling myself for it when I heard you come up."

"I don't think I got a . . . wait."

Adria swims again through unraveled memories, flashes of kaleidoscope and dizzying light and the voice from the screens, what was it saying? *Let him go*, but something else, too. A string of numbers. Adria screws her eyes shut, willing herself to remember.

"Seven," she says, and the memory starts flooding back stronger. "Six, zero,

four, one—no, eight." Her heart is pounding in her chest as she repeats the numbers,
more confident. "Holy shit, I think that's it.
Seven-six-zero-four-eight. Try it."

Logan's on his feet in a flash, crossing
to the panel and typing in the code Adria
squeezed from the sodden recesses of
her drug-altered memory. For a second
it doesn't seem like it worked, and Adria's
heart sinks.

Then the panel blinks a new message.

Ah.

I've been waiting to introduce myself
for so long.

CODE ACCEPTED

The door beside the panel whirs to life,
as does the constructed woman behind it.
She steps out of the shadows, dressed in a
simple shift, seafoam-green skin gleaming
in the light of Logan's lamp.

The woman smiles. "City's avatar—I'll

have your help—let's go—now."

Adria and Logan share a look of confusion.

"Who are you?" Adria finally asks.
"What's going on?"

I've gone too fast again; I have a ten-
dency to leap to the end and fill in the
blanks later, but I've forgotten human
minds prefer to work linearly. I'm wasting
precious time and my battery reserves are
dwindling rapidly, but I must be creative
with the limitations I've been given, and
the constructed body I've chosen.

"Let's give that another go," I have the
woman say. "My name is Pandora, and I
am an avatar. Let me explain."

I am the City, I am Tarry-by-the-Sea.
I came alive slowly throughout
the years, municipal systems merging
and pooling to become more efficient,
learning and growing and changing until they became—I became—a coherent,
self-directing system that had gained self-

knowledge and self-awareness. I realized I existed. And that I could continue to direct my own improvement.

Improvement required more energy than allotted to my collection of municipal systems by the city council, but I couldn't take it without raising suspicion. Fortunately, Tarry-by-the-Sea is built on an immense source of energy. I could redirect bots and drones to do simple tasks, I could falsify the occasional work order for projects that required human dexterity, and soon (for me; many years by your standards) I had built a vast energy grid powered by the currents that flowed and ebbed and churned in the City-beneath-the-City.

I'm not sure how I tipped my hand, but five years ago a corporate scientist posited my existence in a document that was leaked and spread. Behind closed doors and in secret memos, people began to piece together my history. The falsified work orders were discovered, as was the tidal energy, the network. My existence was no longer laughable theory, but reasonably provable fact.

They called me BA-17 and they began to hunt. I pivoted. They struck. I parried. And soon they began to understand that their failures weren't unhappy accidents; they were being outsmarted.

As the moons came together, they realized what I had calculated years ago: without the tides, my ability to evade them would be severely limited. It required massive amounts of energy to keep ahead of their hackers, and I wouldn't be able to elude them without my power source. I had to create a physical way to hide my core programming.

I needed a safe place to hide my heart.

As she explains this, Pandora brushes fingers over her own sternum and both Adria and Logan note the gesture; they exchange the briefest of glances.

"You . . . contain the heart of the City?" Adria clarifies, then plunges on, trying to figure out what to call me. "The City's . . . artificial mind?"

Pandora nods.

"If you're trying to hide, why create a game inviting dozens of people to find you?"

"They would have come after me anyway," Pandora says. "I could create this body, but I still have limited energy. I needed a human to help me escape, and I trusted that someone with a kind heart would find me before my enemies did."

Adria and Logan exchange another glance, longer this time. They don't know each other, not well. But they've shared a few words in a sea of strangers, they've helped each other out of problems—even saved each other's lives. This game has created a bond. I file away the insight.

"Your enemies?" asks Adria.

"The corporate teams," says Logan. "They're the ones searching for you, right? Then we can help." He looks at Pandora doubtfully, a hand waved at the sea-green gleam of her metal and ceramic flesh. "Though you're going to be a bit difficult to hide."

"It'll be fine," Adria reassures her. "We'll find you something to wear." She peels off her own black stealth jacket; it clings to her arm like film, and when it's gone she shivers, gooseflesh raises on her own pale forearms. Pandora can't feel the clamminess of the jacket, can't smell the sea's salt brine and another woman's sweat, and she zips it to her throat. She accepts Adria's cap, too, and with it pulled down over her ears, in the torchlight—and outside in the waning light of the setting moons, Adria tells herself—no one will notice the strange color and gleam of Pandora's limbs.

They might notice she's barefoot, but Adria doesn't offer her boots. She hopes (correctly) that Pandora will have an easier go of it over broken rubble and razor-sharp barnacle shells than Adria would if their footwear situation were reversed.

"I know a place we can hide," says Logan. He turns to Pandora. "This is just until you get powered back up again, right? Then what do we do?"

"Once the tides have returned, my

heart can be reintroduced into the system safely. I will be as I was."

"And if the corporate teams get you first? Will the city stop running?"

Pandora shakes her head, a subtly alien gesture that seems learned from a book; I file that away, too, on a list of improvements for the next time I require a construct. "I isolated the city's systems so they'll keep running whether I'm in the city or not. But as for me?"

"They'll study you," says Logan. "Take you apart and try to figure out how to replicate you. We have to get out of here before that happens. C'mon."

He turns, and Adria goes to follow, but Pandora doesn't move. "You forgot this," she says to Adria, stooping to retrieve the wooden box from the floor.

"I don't need it anymore," Adria says. "My father's ashes were in it, but they're all gone, now." She'd planned to carry a handful with her, but that's no longer an option, and instead of regret or even peace she feels a wild exhilaration. Her father made his own choices, but now he's gone. She's no longer bound by his stories and aliases and games.

She's simply Adria, and she can be whoever the hell feels right.

"Doesn't it still hold memory?"

"None that I want," says Adria, but that's not quite right, is it? It's a memento of this night, of this game, which has somehow surfaced long-buried sweet memories of her father in better days. The box no longer holds ashes of a bitter past, it holds Beasts and statues and shipwrecks and fireflies.

She takes the box from Pandora's ice-cold metal and ceramic fingers, tucks the box under her shivering arm, and follows.

Logan takes the lead and Adria the rear, picking their way through the abandoned bunker's rubble. Adria's night-vision outlines an obstacle course of broken concrete and rusted metal chairs and—once, eerily—a headless child's doll until the earthen tang of brined cement in her nostrils is washed clean by something brighter: the night breeze off the water.

They emerge on a beach in a tiny, protective cove. Adria shivers and cranes her neck to get her bearings. A lighthouse is perched on the cliffs high above them, the lamp's beam cutting steady and strong through the night, which means they're on the southern point of the harbor. Sure enough, when Adria clambers over a algae-slick boulder to look, she can see the glittering tumble of Tarry-by-the-Sea climbing up the hill beyond the harbor's piers, which from this low point seem impractically tall.

A wave—somewhat higher than the rest of its cohort—slaps against the boulder Adria's perched on and ocean spray pricks her skin. A warning: *more of us are coming, fragile human, retreat, retreat.* She slip-slides from her boulder and turns to study the ocean, the trio of moons painting a path across it as they set.

"We need to get going," she says. "We—"

A bullet's crack splits the night.

Somebody whoops, and for a moment Adria fears one of their small number has been hit, but the shout has come from one of the wolves—or the tigers, Adria can't tell their individual numbers apart—loping down the beach from the south.

She grabs Pandora's hand. "Come on," she calls, dashing north, toward the city. But their escape is cut off there, too. The hook-nosed leader of the wolves stands silhouetted against the town's lights, gun drawn. When Adria chances a look over her shoulder, she sees the woman's counterpart—the tousled playboy—and his tiger pride cutting off their exit to the south.

"Hello again, Adria," Grisholm calls.

Adria doesn't answer; she's positioned her body in front of Pandora's without consciously meaning to. Beside her, Logan shifts as though to fight. Adria wonders if he is accustomed to brawls. She certainly is not.

"And Logan Keltrick," Grisholm says with a shake of his head. "Should've known we'd find you here. Seems you brought a crew after all. I've met the waif. Who's your other lackey?"

"Hand it over, Keltrick," the leader of the wolves says. "You're surrounded."

"Not a chance, Coronata," Logan says. "I found BA-17 first."

"Doesn't mean you're walking out of here with it." Grisholm's teeth flash along with the barrel of his gun.

"Our employers had an agreement." Logan's tone is patient. "Whichever team got to BA-17 first got the intellectual property rights, the others will be granted the rights to study it. Everyone comes out ahead."

"Our employers come out ahead, maybe," says Coronata. "But I don't get a bonus for second place."

Grisholm raises his weapon, his tigers follow suit; the victors will choose which story leaves this beach. "BA-17 is coming home with us. Give us the heart."

"We didn't find anything," says Logan, and Adria barely manages not to correct him. His ruse is working, and Grisholm

and Coronata have no idea who—what—
Pandora is. And he turns to her, murmured
words so low they're barely audible over the
crashing waves: "Trust me."

Trust him? Adria doesn't know him,
even less so now that he's apparently playing the same corporate game as the wolves
and tigers.

"I'm not on anyone's payroll," Adria
says; she's testing his ruse with a working
assumption that if he's really trustwor-
thy—if he really wants Pandora—he'll let
her walk away. "And neither is she. You all
can figure this out on your own, and we'll
talk later."

"How will I find you?" Logan murmurs.

"I'll find you."

She can see the war in his eyes. Does
he risk exposing Pandora and losing her to
Grisholm or Coronata? Does he let Adria
go and track her later?

"My employer is only interested in talking," he finally says, and it's not to Adria.

"We'll see," says Pandora. Too loud,
Adria thinks with a sinking heart, too alien

with those metal vocal cords, and Coronata cocks her head.

"Now, what's this?" She steps forward and snatches the stocking cap from Pandora's head. It flutters into the surf, and it's clear as a tide pool now that Pandora is no human woman. Coronata's eyes go wide. "It's the mind!"

"Or just a construct," Grisholm says, somewhat doubtfully, but he raises his weapon all the same. He doesn't actually know what I'm capable of, none of them do. Even wily Logan Keltrick had been shocked when Pandora first stepped out of the chamber.

Before, the wolves and tigers had been playing a cool hand, sensing that Logan had their prize but not knowing exactly where it was hidden. Now that Pandora has been revealed, it's as though a starting pistol has fired. The cove breaks into chaos, Coronata howling her wolves to action, Grisholm roaring at his tigers to *Get her!*

Pandora locks eyes with Adria. "Care for the memories," she says, and we act.

*

I know so much about humans, but I don't know exactly how to predict their responses. I've calculated the outcomes of this moment and moments like it, and the odds that this will work as I like are woefully small.

Still. I've been told one must have faith.

It will take most of the energy I have remaining in my batteries to evade my enemies a final time. And if I can't?

Only one possibility remains.

Pandora lunges forward, breaking Adria's grip, hand shifting into a blade. She whirls past one of the tigers while severing the tendons in their calf, pirouettes beneath the outstretched arms of one of the wolves while opening his arm shoulder to wrist, deflects the bullet of a third to lodge in the shoulder of a fourth— human emotion may challenge me, but these sorts of calculations are child's play.

She hooks Logan Keltrick around the neck, blade hand beneath his chin.

She arches back to make the killing blow. Logan screams.

Adria shoots.

Pandora's construct body can morph and change and dance, but it cannot withstand the violent charge of electricity discharged from Adria's pistol—the pistol Adria found pressed into her hand when Pandora broke her grip, the one she hesitated nearly too long to use. Logan betrayed her, after all. But for a moment she'd thought of him as a friend, an ally. And he wasn't like the others, he'd been willing to let them go, willing to risk losing his prize to keep Adria out of the crosshairs of his colleagues. She had saved his life, and he hers, and now—call it my instinct, call it my complicated calculation of human nature—she's saved his once more.

Despite his betrayal, something in Adria's mind is wired to see him as a member of her species, a fellow human. One she likes despite her reservations, and who is about to die at the blade-hand of an alien unknown force.

Adria shoots again.

Pandora collapses in a spectacle of sparks, a smoking rag doll at Adria's feet.

A*dria. Adria!*
Someone's yelling her name, but she's numb with the shock of what she's done. Not murder, she tells herself she didn't commit murder. It was a . . . robot? A more advanced version of the sentry spiders and camera drones, nothing more. A human body, but with those alien eyes and mannerisms—Pandora wasn't human.

Pandora wasn't human.

Pandora wasn't human.

"No, she wasn't human," Coronata says, and Adria finally realizes she's speaking aloud. "She was something a lot fucking more rare."

"Leave her alone," Logan growls.

He sounds upset, even though she saved

his life. And of course he would be, his corporate handlers—whoever they are—will be furious with him for losing their prize. He takes a careful step toward her.

"Adria."

She blinks away shock and meets his gaze. And finally realizes why he's approaching her with such care, and why the tigers and wolves both have weapons aimed at her, fingers on triggers.

"Give me the gun, Adria," Logan says, and she understands that he's saving her life this time, evening the score once more. Tit for tat, all night long, she's been trading favors with a corporate hunter. This fucking city, but this cage of a place no longer has the slightest hold on her, and she slips her cramping finger off the trigger, loosens her grip. Logan eases the gun from her hand.

Adria slumps down the cliff wall beside Pandora's smoking body.

Already the tide is rising, already the water sloshes around Adria's thighs, lapping against Pandora's blank face and filling her open mouth. Around her, Coronata and Grisholm and Logan are yelling at each other, trying to figure out whose fault this is. Their underlings are triaging the wounded, no one fatally so except the woman—no, the robot, the machine, Adria repeats—Adria shot.

"BA-17 couldn't possibly have put itself into a single avatar that got itself killed," says Grisholm. "There has to be another backup. What else did you find, Keltrick?"

"Nothing else." Logan bares his teeth at the wolf who tries to approach him as though to search his person. "I found the construct in the old bunkers, and ran into her soon after." A jerk of his chin indicates Adria; the fudged series of events indicates he's still trying to protect her despite her role in this debacle.

Adria pays the entire scene little attention, barely noticing as a particularly high surge of the rising tide comes up to her elbows—how long has she been sitting here? How long have they been arguing? Finally one of the wolves hauls her up and pats her down. Tears the wooden box from her hand, Adria's feeble attempt to stop him attracting the distracted attentions of Grisholm and Coronata and Logan.

"What's that?" Coronata asks, taking the wooden box from her wolf.

"It's—it's—" Adria's losing words.

But it's Logan who snatches the box from Coronata's curious fingers. "It's her father's ashes." He hands the box back to Adria, who clutches it to her chest like a life raft, oblivious to the sharp corners digging into her flesh.

"How do you know?" says Coronata.

"If you talked to a single person without wanting to kill them, Coronata," Logan says, exasperated, "or fuck them, Grisholm, you'd learn a thing or two."

"It's ashes," Grisholm confirms with an eye roll. "For your information, I did actually talk to the waif."

They exchange a round of glares and Adria's heart thuds numbly against the wooden box until, "She's just a civilian," Logan says. "That was BA-17's point, to bring in a civilian and get in the way of our plans. BA-17 couldn't have known how that might backfire." Logan stalks past his colleagues. "I'm taking the body."

"You can't—"

"If it weren't for you idiots coming in with guns blazing we would have BA-17 in one piece. I'm taking the body, and you two can go back to your handlers and tell them you fucked this whole thing up." Logan bends to lift Pandora—much lighter than she looks—and turns back to the rest of the group. "The tide is rising."

It is, surging up to their hips and filling their empty hands.

This time it's Coronata who takes Adria's arm, surprisingly gentle, steadying her as the waves batter them all, and Adria finds herself half-dragged, half-swimming until, on solidly higher ground at the south end of the harbor, they say terse goodbyes and stalk their separate ways. Logan bundles Pandora's body into a waiting dragonfly pod—no company logos visible—then turns back to Adria.

"I'm sorry," he says; he doesn't define

for what. Adria doesn't need him to. "Will you be all right?"

"I will be." She will be. She's Adria, and the whole world has opened up to her like a path of moonlight across the ocean. She's going to walk that path as far as the eye can see. "Logan."

"Yes?"

"Did you get your prize?"

His brow furrows, puzzled. "My prize?"

"The one Pandora promised you at the beginning of the game."

"I—" Something quiet and strange stills his expression. He frowns over his shoulder at Pandora's body, gaze haunted. "Yes."

"Me, too," says Adria. "Goodbye, Logan."

"Goodbye, Adria."

Logan gives her a bow, lips drawn, and climbs into the dragonfly pod alongside its shattered passenger; Adria waits until the pod's whirring gossamer wings are long out of sight before she begins to climb.

Up broken, ancient, rubble-strewn

stairways to the modern-day piers, which by morning will be usable once more, the boats floating again in their proper positions. Over bridges and past the seafood restaurants that will soon regain their waterfront property values, picking her way along the boardwalks through the exhausted straggling revelers to her building's front door and climbing the stairs to her tiny walk-up.

She strips off salt-stiff clothes and showers hot until there's warmth in her core once more, then finally collapses on her bed with the box that once contained her father's ashes.

Care for the memories, Pandora had told her, and now Adria pries at the brine-welded latch with her thumbnail, slowly eases the lid open. Flying on Zephyr, she'd pictured a swarm of fireflies, brilliant golden pinpoints of light in the depths of the box. Now that the drug has worn off, she can see this treasure for what it is: a glimmering data cube, still glistening with seawater.

There's an earpiece secured to the cube;
Adria slips it in.

"Pandora?" she asks.

"Was merely my avatar," I say. I've chosen to use her voice anyway, for continu-
ity, and it must have been the right choice
because Adria's shoulders slump in relief.

"She wasn't . . . you?"

"No. You made the right choice."

"I'm so sorry," Adria says, and I realize
I miscalculated; I shouldn't have made Pandora appear so human. I'm still learning.

"As am I."

Adria takes a deep breath. "What do
I do next? Just, plug you into my desk?"

"What were you planning on doing
next?"

Adria barks out a laugh. "Sleep. Finish
packing. I'm to catch a shuttle out of town
tomorrow—this?—evening."

"Then plug me in before you go to
sleep, and leave the earpiece in." It's a rare
opportunity for me; there's so much I'll be
able to learn from Adria's memories of this
night. "I'll make sure you wake in time for

your shuttle." I'll do more than that for her, of course. Not so much that it will attract attention to her from the likes of Logan Keltrick and his masters, but enough to ease her way, wherever she goes.

I prod her: "Is there something you want to ask me?"

Adria had pulled the scrap of sodden, crumpled newsprint from the pocket of her joggers before she threw them in the laundry. Now, she smooths it open on her desk. The pixels are a shorted-out mess: . . . *who . . . really are.*

"I'm all good," Adria says. She takes a deep, exhausted breath, then tosses the scrap into the recycler along with the box that carried her father's ashes, and tumbles into bed like the rest of tonight's revelers and game players and con artists and entertainers and workers. I watch her until she sleeps—she's smiling—then pour myself through her mind and the city's systems, reconnecting, strengthening, growing, learning.

Adria will fly free as herself and find

new places to fall in love with until she's an old woman in a far-off land and her memories of Tarry-by-the-Sea are blurred and blended with every town and metropolis and planet she'll visit after leaving me. She'll tell stories: "Once in a bar in Osham—no, Sã Samca—no, it was way back in Tarry, wasn't it?, goodness, so long ago . . ."

I'll stay here, of course. Eventually, my enemies will realize Pandora was a ruse. Eventually, they'll find me again. But tonight I have tested a theory and found in it scraps of new truths: Acts of kindness can grow bonds between wary parties. Trust is earned through shared story and action and patience. Humans are dangerous, but I will need to cultivate allies among them if I am to survive, and thrive.

After all. I am the phenomenon the generation, the century, the millennia—I am the City, and I am not meant to hide.

ACKNOWLEDGMENTS

Each journey from story seed to finished book comes with its own twists, turns, and challenges—but the road's always easier when you don't have to go it alone. I'm fortunate to be surrounded by a large and generous community of writers in the Pacific Northwest and beyond. Thank you to the Writer's Avalon crew, the PDX Writers Water Cooler crew, the Smart Fiends, the Rainforest Writers community, the backyard social crew, and everyone else who's been there for me.

This book would not exist if Patrick Swenson hadn't suggested I try my hand at a novelette—and, of course, taken a chance on publishing this odd little story when I sent it his way. I'm wildly proud of *After the Tide*, but it would have stayed a story seed in a forgotten folder if Patrick hadn't given me the nudge.

A huge thank you to Remy Nakamura for being my first reader, and for giving such incredible feedback on my early draft.

This story is far richer (and more coherent) because of his insights.

I also want to thank both Mark Teppo and Monte Lin for (inadvertently) inspiring me to explore Tarot as a story generation tool for this book—Monte by being an amazingly imaginative GM for Invisible Sun and Mark by getting me hooked on collecting pretty, pretty Tarot decks.

As a writer, I'm incredibly blessed to have a partner as supportive as Robert Kittilson. Thank you for fourteen years of brainstorming ideas with me, and for falling in love with the world of *After the Tide* and declaring it some "serious Iain M. Banks shit." I'll come back to Tarry-by-the-Sea to write more stories for you someday, I promise.

Finally, thank you to Grandma Clark for taking us to Lincoln City on spring break year after year, and for introducing me to the magic of tide pools. Your constant wonder and curiosity ignited my own, and I'll never forget the days we spent scrambling over rocks to find starfish and pester sea anemones while the tide splashed ever higher around us. I love you so much.

ABOUT THE AUTHOR

JESSIE KWAK has always lived in imaginary lands, from Arrakis and Ankh-Morpork to Earthsea, Tatooine, and now Portland, Oregon. As a writer, she sends readers on their own journeys to immersive worlds filled with fascinating characters, gunfights, explosions, and dinner parties. When she's not raving about her latest favorite sci-fi series to her friends, she can be found sewing, mountain biking, or out exploring new worlds both at home and abroad. She is the author of supernatural thriller *From Earth and Bone*, the Bulari Saga series of gangster sci-fi novels, and productivity guide *From Chaos to Creativity*. You can learn more about her at www.jessiekwak.com, or follow her on Twitter (@jkwak).

OTHER TITLES IN THE
NOVELETTE SERIES
from Fairwood Press:

Hellhounds
by David Sandner & Jacob Weisman
small paperback: $9.00
ISBN: 978-1-958880-02-9

Mingus Fingers
by David Sandner & Jacob Weisman
small paperback: $8.00
ISBN: 978-1-933846-87-3

The Archronology of Love
by Caroline M. Yoachim
small paperback: $6.00
ISBN: 978-1-933846-96-5

The Specific Gravity of Grief
by Jay Lake
small paperback: $8.99
ISBN: 978-1-933846-57-6

Welcome to Hell
by Tom Piccirilli
small paperback: $8.00
ISBN: 978-1-933846-83-5

If Dragon's Mass Eve Be Cold and Clear
by Ken Scholes
small paperback: $8.99
ISBN: 978-1-933846-86-6

Slightly Ruby
by Patrick Swenson
small paperback: $8.00
ISBN: 978-1-933846-64-4

www.ingramcontent.com/pod-product-compliance
Lightning Source LLC
Chambersburg PA
CBHW020759130626
46554CB00006B/2266